Ah-CHOO!

To Elias — M.C.

For Jules and Jim, from Pops — B.M.

Go to scholastic.com for web site information
on Scholastic authors and illustrators.

Text copyright © 2002 by Margery Cuyler.
Illustrations copyright © 2002 by Bruce McNally.
All rights reserved. Published by Scholastic Inc.
SCHOLASTIC, CARTWHEEL BOOKS, and associated logos are
trademarks and/or registered trademarks of Scholastic Inc.

Library of Congress Cataloging-in-Publication Data

Cuyler, Margery.
     Ah-choo! / by Margery Cuyler; illustrated by Bruce McNally.
     p. cm.
     "Cartwheel books."
     Summary: A sneeze spreads from a farmer to his wife to various animals
on the farm until they are all in bed with the flu.
     ISBN 0-439-26618-1 (pbk.)
     [1. Sneezing--Fiction. 2. Domestic animals--Fiction. 3. Influenza--Fiction.] I. McNally, Bruce, ill.
     II. Title. PZ7.C997 Ah 2002
        [E]--dc21   2001020756

10 9 8 7 6 5 4 3   02 03 04 05 06

Printed in the U.S.A.   24
First printing, March 2002

Ah-CHOO!

by Margery Cuyler
Illustrated by Bruce McNally

SCHOLASTIC INC.

New York   Toronto   London   Auckland   Sydney
Mexico City   New Delhi   Hong Kong   Buenos Aires

Ah . . .   Ah . . .   Ah . . .

Oh, no.

Ah . . .   Ah . . .   Ah . . .

Bow-wow.

Ah . . .   Ah . . .   Ah . . .

Moo-moo.

Ah . . .   Ah . . .   Ah . . .

Oink-oink.

Ah . . .   **Ah . . .**   **Ah . . .**

Hoot-hoot.

Ah . . .   Ah . . .   Ah . . .

Bah-bah.

Ah . . . Ah . . . Ah . . .

CHOO!

Cluck-cluck.

Ah . . .   Ah . . .   Ah . . .

Peep-peep.

Ah . . .   Ah . . .   Ah . . .

Do you have the flu?

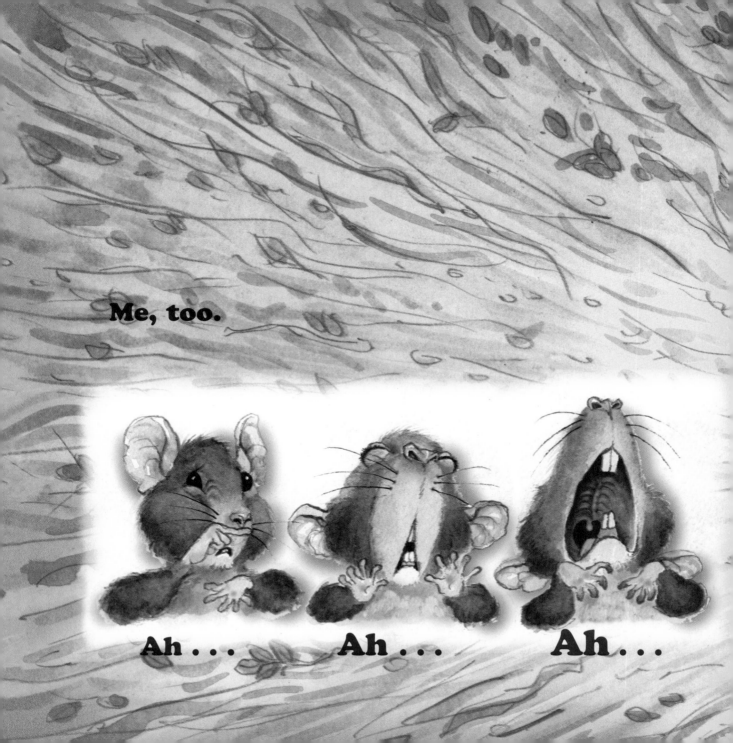

CHOO!

Ah . . .   Ah . . .   Ah . . .

CHOO!